For Kat

"L'enfant Entitled"
Story and words by Owen Fitzgeoffrey
Illustrations by J.E. Larson

Published by
Antimatter Publishing
Redmond, WA
www.antimatterpublishing.com

Once, there was a unique and special little boy.

He never had to ask for a single thing.

And what things he had!

He had shooting toys...

Shouting toys...

Fighting toys..

Driving toys...

...and flying toys.

Smartphones.

Devices.

And video games.

In fact, the very unique and special boy had EVERY video game and was the video game champion of the whole house!

But one day, all that changed.

You see, the boy invited his friend over to play video games and something happened that had never happened before.

The boy LOST!

And losing was not unique. Or special!

"You didn't really lose, dear," said his mother.

"You just didn't win, that one time! You are still very unique, and very special!"

But the boy did not feel special.

He did not feel special *at all*.

"You know what will make you feel right again," she said. "We'll get something special to eat, something just for you."

"Fine!" he said.

So off they went in their great big car.

"The temperature on my electrically heated leather seat is TOO WARM," he complained.

He was so incensed he could barely bring himself to watch cartoons on the headrest monitor.

And he scarcely believed his eyes when they arrived at the FAST FOOD restaurant.

"This is not special! Take me to the special coffee shop instead!"

"I want a special breakfast sandwich, one with organic free range eggs, artisanal black pepper bacon, and caved-aged gruyere cheese!"

At the special coffee shop, he watched suspiciously as the barista placed his special sandwich in a microwave oven.

When it was ready, he took one single bite.

"This is COLD IN THE MIDDLE," he yelled at the barista.

Then he threw it on the floor where it belonged.

His mother quickly ordered him a croissant.

"This isn't FLAKY ENOUGH!"

...and on the floor it went.

Finally, his mother ordered him a hot chocolate.

"This isn't REAL COCOA!"

...and on the floor it went too.

A kindly old wizard waited in the line. He
watched the boy's predicament with interest.

"My boy," said the kindly old wizard.

"I see you are making quite the mess. My magical wand can help clean it up!"

The unique and special little boy snatched the magical wand from the kindly old wizard's hand.

"Oh!" said the kindly old wizard. "You are keen!"

"Go ahead and point my magical wand at whatever you need to disappear. Wish it to be gone, and gone it shall be!"

The boy pointed the magical wand at the mess on the floor.

"I want it to go – AWAY!"

Just like that, the mess disappeared in a puff of magical smoke.

"Well done lad, you've got the knack!" said the kindly old wizard.

He held out his hand to take back the magical wand, but the boy refused to return it.

You see, the magical wand made the boy feel very unique and special indeed.

"I say!" said the kindly old wizard.

"Keep my magical wand if you must. But be careful! You are just a little boy, and the magical wand has much magical power!"

The boy's mother was relieved that he was starting to feel special again.

"I'll take you shopping for something extra special and unique," she said.

"Then you will be back to your old special self!"

"How about a special new shooting toy?"

But when he looked at the shooting toys, the boy noticed
that other children could buy the exact same thing.

The shooting toys were not unique or special at all!

He took out the magical wand and pointed it.

"I want them to go - AWAY!"

And the shooting toys disappeared in a puff of magical smoke.

"Oh! Well perhaps a special new flying toy will have you feeling special once again!"

Once again, the boy noticed that other children could buy the exact same toys.

These were not special flying toys at all!

"I want them all to go – AWAY!" he shouted.

And just like that, the flying toys disappeared.

When he looked at the noisy toys, he saw the same thing.

Just anyone could have them!

These were not special noisy toys at all!

"I already have every new video game," he shouted.

"AWAY!"

"And I already have every new tablet and every new phone!"

"AWAY!"

No matter where his mother took him there
was nothing that made the boy feel special.

Then he realized what the problem was.

"MOTHER," he shouted.

"YOU are not making me feel special AT ALL!"

And just like that, his mother disappeared
in a tiny puff of magical smoke.

The boy pointed the magical wand at the housewares department.

"AWAY!"

Then he pointed the magical wand at the dog food and cat food.

"AWAY!"

He turned the magical wand to the ladies' underpants department.

"AWAY!"

"AWAY! AWAY! AWAY," the boy yelled. He screwed up his eyes,
twirled the magical wand around and around, and shouted,

"EVERYTHING! THE WHOLE WORLD! THE WHOLE
UNIVERSE!"

"AWAY, AWAY, AWAY!"

A huge cloud of magical smoke covered everyting...

...then drifted away.

All that remained was the great void of nothingness.

The boy sat and pondered in the great void of nothingness.

He pondered for a very long time.

Then he had a very good idea.

"WIZARD," he shouted.

"WIZARD! Come here NOW!"

"Oh, look how well you've used my magical wand!" said the kindly old wizard. "Everything is gone. Not a single thing remains! You must be very pleased. Very pleased indeed!"

The boy frowned, and pushed out his lip as far as it would go.

"NO!" He shouted. "I am not pleased at all! There is nothing left for me to send away!"

The kindly old wizard rested his wrinkled hand upon
his wrinkled chin and considered for a moment.

"Ah, I see what's wrong. When there is nothing,
there is nothing for you to send away!"

The boy pouted as fiercely as he could. "Yes," he scowled. "Make me something else to send away!"

Just then a twinkle appeared in the wizard's eye.

"Oh," he said. "Don't you know that my magical wand also has magic to create anything you can imagine!"

"Go ahead, lad! Just use your imagination to think of whatever pleases you, point the wand, and POOF! There it shall be!"

The boy wasn't sure what an imagination was,
so he waved the magical wand around a little.

All that appeared was a tiny puff of smoke.

"Go ahead, my boy," said the kindly old wizard.

"What is the one thing that will make you feel special?"

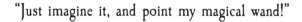

"Just imagine it, and point my magical wand!"

The boy tried very hard to do what the kindly old wizard had told him to do.

No matter how hard he tried, he couldn't make a single thing appear.

"This wand is BROKEN," he shouted.

"I WANT THIS WAND TO GO..."

"OH NO, DEAR LAD," cautioned the kindly old wizard.

"Do not send the magical wand away!"

"Why, the magical wand and your imagination are the only two things that can bring the whole universe back!"

"FINE," cried the boy.

"Then I want you, WIZARD, to go..."

"AWAY!"

"How very sad," said the kindly old wizard.

"If you wish me to go, then I shall go. But before I do, allow me to give you a gift!"

"Keep my magical wand. One day you will discover your imagination, and you will feel very special indeed!"

The boy thought about the kindly old wizard's words.

He tried very hard to think of all the things
that had made him feel so special before.

But his mind was as empty as the great void of nothingness.

Finally, he saw what the problem really was.

"MAGICAL WAND," the boy shouted.

"I WANT YOU TO GO..."

"AWAY!"

The boy was finally unique.

And special.

In fact, he was so unique and so special, he was the only thing that existed.

After some time had passed - or perhaps none at all - the boy thought he heard a raven.

"COME HERE RAVEN," he shouted. "Come here RIGHT NOW!"

But there was no raven.

And the unique and special little boy sat
in the great void of nothingness for a very...

...very long while, indeed.

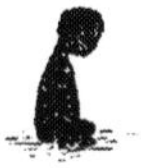

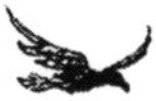

LA FIN

Made in the USA
San Bernardino, CA
08 December 2016